Orange Porange

by Howard Pearlstein

Illustrated by Rob Hardison

Marshall Cavendish Children

For Debi, All my love, always. — Howard

For Sara, my muse, and Frances, my smile. — Rob

Red, Bread!

Orange... Rorange?

"Orange... Porange?"

"Pink, Wink!"

Orange… Grrrorange!

Gray, Hay!

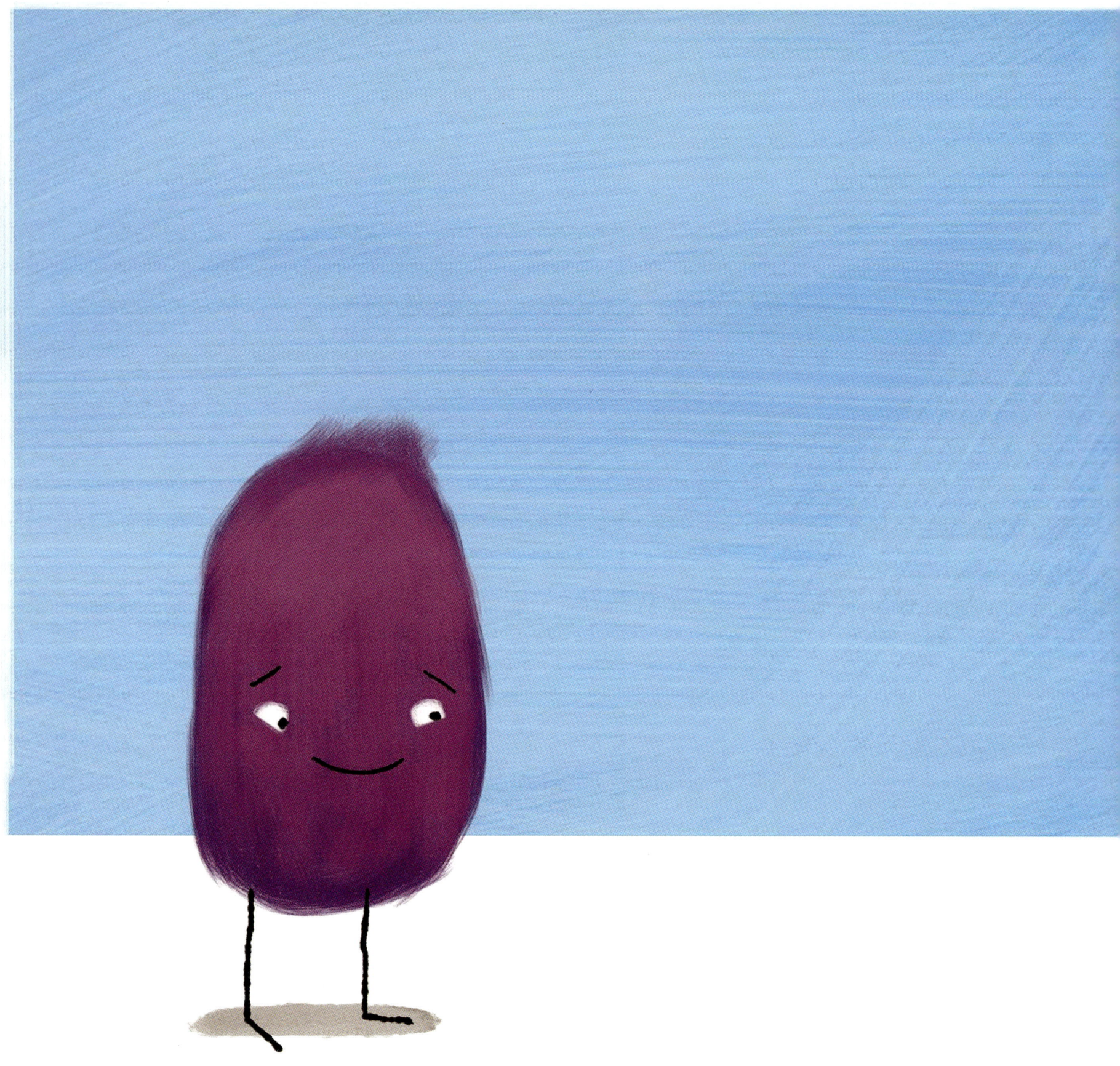

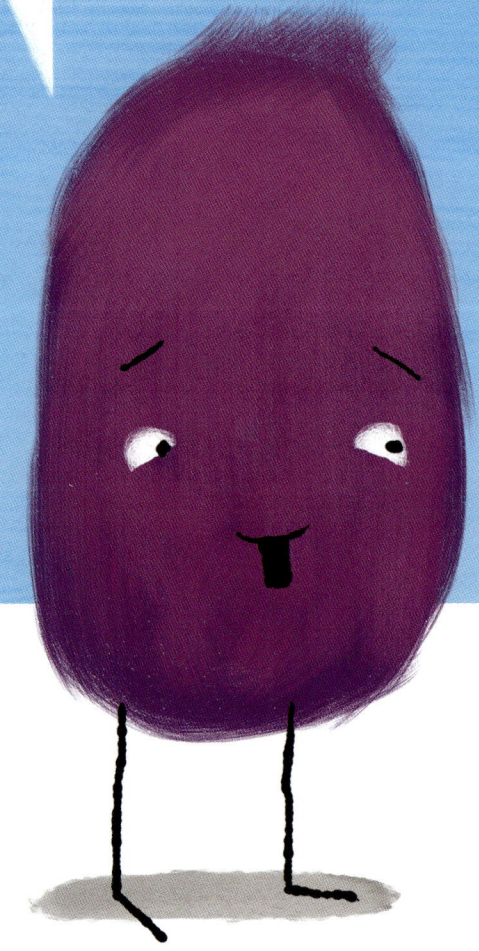

Text © 2021 Howard Pearlstein
Illustrations © 2021 Rob Hardison

First published 2021
Paperback edition 2022

ISBN 978-981-48-6893-8 (Hardcover Edition)
ISBN 978-981-5044-83-6 (Paperback Edition)

Published by Marshall Cavendish Children
An imprint of Marshall Cavendish International

All rights reserved

No part of this publication may be reproduced, stored in a retrieval system or transmitted, in any form or by any means, electronic, mechanical, photocopying, recording or otherwise, without the prior permission of the copyright owner. Requests for permission should be addressed to the Publisher, Marshall Cavendish International (Asia) Private Limited, 1 New Industrial Road, Singapore 536196. Tel: (65) 6213 9300 E-mail: genref@sg.marshallcavendish.com Website: www.marshallcavendish.com

The publisher makes no representation or warranties with respect to the contents of this book, and specifically disclaims any implied warranties or merchantability or fitness for any particular purpose, and shall in no event be liable for any loss of profit or any other commercial damage, including but not limited to special, incidental, consequential, or other damages.

Other Marshall Cavendish Offices:
Marshall Cavendish Corporation, 800 Westchester Ave, Suite N-641, Rye Brook, NY 10573, USA
• Marshall Cavendish International (Thailand) Co Ltd, 253 Asoke, 16th Floor, Sukhumvit 21 Road, Klongtoey Nua, Wattana, Bangkok 10110, Thailand • Marshall Cavendish (Malaysia) Sdn Bhd, Times Subang, Lot 46, Subang Hi-Tech Industrial Park, Batu Tiga, 40000 Shah Alam, Selangor Darul Ehsan, Malaysia.

Marshall Cavendish is a registered trademark of Times Publishing Limited

Printed in Singapore